HATS OFF TO THE HARTS!

Suburban life will never be the same after you've met the Harts. Cartoonist Rich Torrey takes an outrageously funny look at life beyond the city limits, where anything can happen . . . and does! So take Hart, you'll love 'em!

MORE BIG LAUGHS

AMERICAN HARTLAND

Rich Torrey

A SIGNET BOOK

NEW AMERICAN LIBRARY

6

7

8

9

10

12

13

14

15

20

21

23

26

28

29

32

33

35

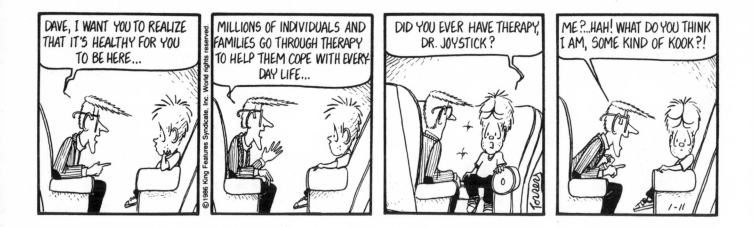

36

38

39

40

42

46

49

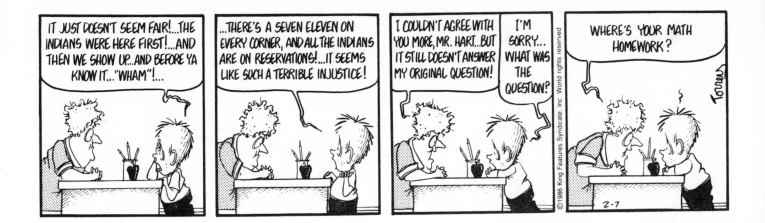

51

56

57

58

64

67

71

73

74

78

81

83

90